In Parvati Education UNIVERSITY

"Entry Gate" Navya is entering the co...
are looking curious about something. What's happening here?

Students: Did you hear what happened in our college today?
Not sure, who did this and what happened yesterday? We all should be aware of our surroundings.
We feel not safe.

Navya got confused that what's happening. She thought to go directly to the Hostel.

In Hostel, everybody is crowded in front of one room. She is going to the crowded room to see why people gathered all together and get really shocked what she saw. Someone laid down on the floor and blood flowing all around.

What could be happened in that room yesterday?

3 MONTHS AGO...............

Navya: What a beautiful day, everything looks so perfect.

Shruti: Come on navya, we all need to work together.

Navya: Yeah, I am coming. After all it's our college fest today.

Amit: Hey you both girls, help us to carry all these gifts.

Shruti: Do we give gifts to all seniors?

Amit: Yes.

Shruti: I have heard that a new student will come today. He is actually transferred from different college. I have also heard that he is little different.
Some say that he is shy, or other says he is flirty. What kind of guy is he?

Navya: You? Shouldn't we just focus on our work? Come on guys, we have a lot of responsibility today. A lot of work is there.

Shruti: You innocent girl always think about work. Let's have some fun too after all it's our college fest today.

Amit: You both still are talking, let's work all together.

Fest begins............................

Shruti: All looks so beautiful, but when a new student will come? waiting.............

Navya: You will never act normal.

Shruti: Let's dance...................

Music goes on.................

Dance and dance...........

Seniors: We will play a game. In this game two names will show, and they need to dance together "Romantic Dance."

Shruti: Ohh, he is here "Looking So Handsome" I wish can get name with her.

Navya: Let's just enjoy.

Senior: Our first two name came and they are Karan and Navya. Both please came on the stage.

Shruti: Yeah navya, you get so lucky to get chance to dance with him. So his name is Karan.

Navya: Oh seriously, why my name need to come up, I will not join.

Shruti: Yeah come on, Let's have fun. We need to respect the senior too.

Seniors: Both karan and Navya, please come on the stage.

On The Stage...

Karan give his hand to navya for dance, at first navya hesitate but accept karan's offer and ready to dance with him.

While dancing...........

Karan: I have never seen you in the college.

Navya: You are a new student, definitely not aware of various faces. Isn't that?

Karan: True, I must started to remember everyone. I will make sure to remember your beautiful face.

Navya: You don't need to remember everybody's face specially mines.

Karan: I think you don't want to dance with me.

Navya: I think, we have dance enough.

She truns around and her scarf got tangled in his button both become stuck at that moment without realizing that she can't left now so she tries to move forward but got stuck again then she looked back at him and both eyes looks each other without any thoughts in a mind.

Navya: It must get tangled while dancing.

She tries to pull back her scarf but more she tries, more get closer to each other.

Karan: Let me help you.

He becomes closer to her while helping without looking at her, navya get more nervous and pull hard, get her scarf and run away.

Karan keeps looking at her because she ran away without saying anything.

Karan: Did she get angry because of me, but I haven't said anything?

Seniors: Now it's turn for other names..........

Party going on

Shruti: Hey navya, why you came back from the stage?

Navya: Nothing, I told you he is kind of flirty guy. Why did I dance with him?

Shruti: Navya, Every handsome guys are flirty........ Hehehe

Navya: Hmm as always what you say. You must really fall for him, but I am not.

Shruti: How could I fall for him without your permission after all you are my best friend. Best friend's advice matter most.

Amit: Hey, girls, let's enjoy all together.

Next Day In College...

Shruti: Hey navya, your bracelet looking beautiful. Where from you purchased? I also want to try too.

Navya: Sure try this (She took off the bracelet and gives her to shruti.)

Shruti: Wow, it's looking beautiful on me. I also want same. May I have this one?

Navya: Sure, you look more beautiful on this.

Shruti: Thanks Navya.

Amit: Hey girls, yesterday party was just so amazing. Oh Shruti, your bracelet looking beautiful.

Shruti: Thanks Amit.

(Karan leads to Library room.)

Hey guys I am going to library room.

Navya: Ok

Amit: Then navya and me going to classroom.

In The Library..

Shruti is standing on library ladder to get books from shelf when Karan is passing in the library.

Shruti: Hey Karan, Can you help me with this ladder to get down.

Karan: Sure (Karan helps shruti to get down from the ladder.)

Shruti: Thank you for your help.

(She is talking while placed her hand on the ladder as her support.)

By the way, what are you doing here? You must be in the classroom. I was just asking.

Karan: Actually whenever I want to read books so mostly time I skipped class.

Shruti: Ok you like reading? Let's go the classroom together. I know your classroom is on a way of my classroom.

Karan: Yes, I like reading alot but now I am here to submit some books not for reading. I am going earlier today because I have my part time job so I think I can't join class today.

Shruti: Ok (She intentionally moves the ladder back with legs and lose the support of ladder and pretend to slip.)

Oh............

Karan: (Catch shruti before she got slipped.)

Are you okay?

Shruti: Thanks again to save me. I got almost slip.

I will retun your favour hehe................

Any help you need then just call my name Shruti at my classroom. I will be there for you hehe...........

Karan: Sure, I will remember you are trying to flirt with me hehe..........

Shruti: Oh, you are too clever.

Karan: Now I need to go for my part time. Let's meet another time at the library, sorry for going earlier.

Shruti: No problem, continue your work.

In the classroom................................

Navya: Where were you navya. Class almost started.

Shruti: Just got a chance to talk with Karan.

Navya: You are still with him hehe.............

Shruti: Yeah now help me with study.

Navya: Sure.

At the Lunch Time...............................

Amit: What a boring class was it. Let's do some fun.

Shruti: I was also thinking the same. Yeah, I have idea let's do night out all together.

Amit: Wow, that's great idea. Let's meet tonight.

Shruti: Navya you also need to come with us. We will go have fun.

Navya: Sure but will not stay too late.

Shruti: No problem. So we will meet tonight in the nearby garden. Okay?

Amit and Navya: Ok. Let's meet tonight.

At The Night...

Amit: Hey girls, you both are looking so beautiful.

Shruti: Thanks but navya your scarf does not suit you. See, it suits me more.

Navya: You are fashion idiol then you must have it.

Shruti: Thanks navya but don't give everything to me otherwise I can get whatever you deserve hehe..........

I was just kidding, you are too innocent navya.

Navya: I know you are kidding... I haven't taken this seriously because you are best friend.

Amit: One second, I have very important call. I think, I will not able to join you guys... I am too sorry, need to go. Let's meet tomorrow at college.

Shruti And Navya: No problem.

Amit went....................

Navya: Yaa, Why karan is coming here? Did you invite him?

Shruti: Yes. I have invited him... Isn't he looking too handsome?

Navya: Why is he here? Come on, what he will do here?

Shruti: Yaa, It will be fun if he is here, amit is not here anyway so we should have someone and I wanted karan to be with us.

Navya: Do whatever you want.

Karan: Hey girls, Navya you are looking beautiful.

Shruti: What about me then?

Karan: You are always outstanding in any dress.

Shruti: So Sweet.

Navya: I think, we are missing soft drinks with us.

Karan: Hey shruti, This is first time I am spending time with you both so I have prepared some present for you both. Would you please bring that present here, It's in the car. You will love it shruti.

Shruti: Sure, I will love it.

Navya: Then I will bring soft drinks for us.

Shruti: Then we will meet here. Karan wait for us.

Shruti went to bring present.

Karan: Should I go with you navya to help you?

Navya: No need to help... It's ok.

Navya went to bring soft drinks.

Navya: Why are you coming with me karan.

Karan: I told you to help you.

Navya: Whatever...........
Ah, It hurts.

Karan: I told, you must be careful while walking. See you hurt your toe.

Navya: I am ok, you don't need to worry.

Karan: You stay here, I will go and buy soft drinks.

(Karan went to the shop to get soft drinks.)

Karan: Here take your soft drinks.

Navya: I told you I am ok, I could also go with you.

Karan: I told you, you must take care of yourself.

Navya: You don't need to take care of myself.

Karan: Would you please talk to me nicely and sorry for any misunderstanding before.

Navya: I am not angry then why you are sorry, you don't need to be sorry.

Karan: Thank god, you are not angry. Can I ask you something? I am very curious to know.

Navya: Sure.

Karan: If I will say that I will like you so much from the first time we met each other eyes, I have just fallen for you and want to know you better than before. Will you allow me to know yourself?

Navya: What are you talking about? You like me.

Karan: I don't like your expression you must be happy to know that most handsome guy likes you.

Navya: What?

Karan: Yaa, don't be angry, I was just kidding. Your reaction was just funny.

Navya: That's why I ignored you, you always flirt.

Karan: Oh sorry, I was just kidding.

Navya: It's ok, shruti must be waiting for us.

Shruti: Did you both went together? You both late.

Karan: Yes, I just thought to help navya. Did you see the present?

Shruti: Oh, I just love it. Thank you so much karan to bring lots of chocalate for us.

Karan: I know you like chocolates so just thought to give chocolates treat to you both. Navya, you will also like it.

Shruti: Navya is not big fan of chocolates as I am, I will surely enjoy it. Thanks.

Karan: Oh most welcome.

Navya: I will enjoy my soft drink. Let's take your soft drinks too and hope we three will spend good time together without any trouble.

Shruti: Why will we have any trouble?

Karan: May she doubt me?

Shruti: Oh no, she must be kidding. Aren't you navya?

Navya: Let's enjoy.

Navya, shruti and karan enjoyed night out all together with dance and singing..........

Next Morning In The College................................

In The Library...

Karan: It's so quiet today in the library.
What's this? "This book belongs to Karan"
Is this book for me?
Let's check what is this.................

(On the pages of the book)

You are very special to me, the way you smile it always makes me think abou you. Should I fell for you or not?
But I have Decided that no matter what other say about you, I have already fallen for you.
"I Like You Karan".

Karan: Who wrote all this on this book?

Shruti: Calling Karan...........

Karan: (Turns back and see shruti standing with flowers.)
Is this you shruti?

Shruti: Have you already read my feeling about you on this book?

Karan: Why do you like me?

Shruti: You are handsome guy, Handsome guy look best always with the beautiful girl. Am I, not beautiful girl? Don't you think if we both will be the couple, other will jealous of us?

Karan: What are you saying shruti?

Shruti: Hey, you get serious. I was just kidding.

You asked suddenly why I like you just make feel nervous. I like you because you look always good to me. Everything is just awesome about you that just can't stop thinking about you.
Will you accept my propasal?

Karan: Yes I Like You Too.

(Thinking on his mind: Even as a joke she is right we both as a couple can make jealous anyone. I will make navya jealous of us until she will not like me because I like navya only. Sorry to use you shruti.)

In The Evening.............................

Navya: Oh Shruti you are looking so happy. What happened?

Shruti: I need to tell you something just waiting for someone.

Navya: Oh then tell us later. Is that really something important?

Shruti: Yes I think you as my bestfriend should know this. Just wait for a while.

Karan: Hey shruti, Why did you call me here?

Shruti: I feel navya should know about us.

Navya: What I should know about you both? Tell me.

Shruti: Navya, actually we both are in relationship. It just happened quickly so I feel you as my best friend should know about this. I know you have some misunderstanding about Karan but trust me he is a good guy.

Navya: I didn't expect this but if you say that you trust him then I am happy for both of you. Congratulation.

Shruti And Karan: Thank you dear.

Karan: I thought navya you would look surprised but you look all fine. I think we both feel relief that you know everything about us. But we both request please don't tell about us to everyone because we don't want rumors.

Shruti: Yes navya. We both decides that we will not tell anyone because you know very well how college students are like. I hope you will understand.

Navya: Don't worry I will not tell anyone about you both.

Shruti: Wow karan you looking so handsome today. We both look just great together. If you and navya would as a couple, It wouldn't look that amazing because our navya know how to look nice but not beautiful.......... Hehehe I am just kidding. don't mind navya.

Karan: Hey, don't tease navya like that she is just innocent.

Navya: I don't mind because I know she is just kiiding.

Shruti: Navya is always too innocent.

Karan: Hey shruti I was thinking to spend sometime in library. Shall we go together?
(Karan intentionally left his mobile phone there.)

Shruti: Let's go dear. Byee navya.
(Both karan and shruti went for library.)

After That................

Navya notice that karan left his mobile phone.

Navya: Karan left his mobile phone. I should inform shruti about this.
Why shruti is not picking her call.
What I will do with this mobile phone. Should I wait for tomorrow but if Karan has some important call to wait. Should I go there? Yeah just go and give his mobile phone to him.

In THe Library...

Shruti: We are here in your favorite place, I guess. Why you love books Karan?

Karan: Books are only place where you can distinguish between reality and illusion.

Shruti: Then what is reality and illusion about love?

Karan: You know you love someone but other person loves you back is always question. May be other person loves you back is your illusion.

Shruti: What about our love? Is it reality or illusion?

Karan: In this case try to find out your answer. Then Karan pull shruti towards him, slightly touch her cheeks and be more closer to her, slowly karan try to kiss her but at that moment navya say "Hey".

Navya: Ah actually Karan forget his mobile there. I thought, maybe he would have some urgent call. Sorry. I think I should not be here.

Shruti: You already spoiled our time.

Karan: It's Ok I am actually waiting for some call from my part time work. Thank you navya to come here (Karan's thoughts: I know navya, you would come here that's why I intentionaly forget my mobile there. I really want to make you feel jealous. Are you jealous right now?)

Shruti: If Karan have some urgent call then it's ok, you have came here.

Navya: I think, I should go now.

Karan: Let me put back this book in shelf. Then go all together because I need to go to my part time job too.

Shruti: Ok
Then suddenly shelf fall on Shruti. Hopefully shruti got aware and moved away from there but got hurt.

Navya: Are you okay navya? your hand look injured.

Shruti: I am okay. I think I got some minor injuries.

Karan: How this shelf fell. Look at yourself shruti you get injured. Let's go to hospital.

Shruti: I also think. Let's go then.

Navya: You both go together. I will manage all this books here.
(Karan and Shruti went to hospital.)

Next Day In The Hospital..

Navya: How are you feeling shruti?

Shruti: I am Ok now.

Karan: You should take care of yourself shruti.

Shruti: Thank you karan, because you are taking care of me, I am feeling much better now.
See, I told you navya, Karan is good boy.

Navya: Thank you karan for taking care of her.

Karan: Don't you have anyone special in your life navya? I am sure you have someone in your heart.

Shruti: Who are you talking about? Look at her. Navya is so boring personality even if she will with someone. I am sure he will easily get bore and do the breakup with her after all she is no fun.

(Navya almost get tears in her eyes and went away from there.)

Karan: Why you need to say something like that to navya. Look at her what you did.

She went away.

(Karan went from there to search navya.)

In The Terrace...

Karan: Are you Ok navya?

Navya: Why are you here? I want to be alone.

Karan: Why do you need to be alone always? Have you ever seen around you? May be, someone is waiting for you.

Navya: What are you talking about? Don't you get it? I want to be alone, Just go.

Karan: I will not go anywhere. I will be here with you because I worry about you. Dam it. I care about you.

Navya: Why do you care about me? You don't need to be.

Karan: I care about you, and I will always care about you because I like you. Don't you get that?

Navya: What but you like shruti. Isn't that?

Karan: I have pretended to like her to make you feel jealous but I was wrong. You even didn't care what I felt about you.

Shruti: What just you said right now. You don't like me but you like navya.

Navya: I am sure shruti, there is some misunderstanding.

Karan: Wait navya, Listen shruti whatever you heard it's true. I have never liked you. Look at you how you behave to others how could I like someone like you?

Navya: Why karan you are doing this?

Karan: It's true navya that I like you. Shruti need to know that. I am going now and shruti don't ever call to me.

(Karan went from there.)

Shruti: Look navya what you did. All happened because of you.

Navya: Are you mad what I did? I have already told you karan is not trustworthy.

Shruti: Stop it. Karan is only mine. Do you get navya.

Navya: Do whatever you want. I am going.

Shruti: Just go but remember it I will make karan mine in anyway.

(Shruti went to her hostel.)

Next Day In The College..
(Present Day)

Students: Did you hear what happened in our college today?
Not sure, who did this and what happened yesterday? We all should be aware of our surroundings.
We feel not safe.

Navya got confused that what's happening. She thought to go directly to the Hostel.

In Hostel, everybody is crowded in front of one room. She is going to the crowded room to see why people gathered all together and get really shocked what she saw. Someone laid down on the floor and blood flowing all around.

Navya shout a loud............... Shruti what you did to yourself. How could you cut your nerves? Please Call ambulance.

Teacher: Move aside everyone. She's already dead still let her move to the Hospital and call police too.

In The Hospital................................

Navya: How is shruti? She is ok.

Doctor: Sorry but she is already dead. We are waiting for police to come.

Navya: How could she just die like this? She didn't care about anyone.

Police Came To The Hospital....................................

Mr Vijay (Police officer): How do you belong to her?

Navya: I am her classmate and best friend too.

Mr Vijay (Police officer): Ok do have any doubt for anyone?

Navya: Not really sir. Last time we just fought.

Mr Vijay (Police officer): You need to come to the police station for helping this investigation. Now shruti's body will go for postmortem.

Navya: Sure Sir.

In The Police Station................................

Mr Vijay (Police officer): What did find in the postmortem.

Mr Aksh(Police): It looks like she cut her nerves. It looks like suicide.

Mr Vijay (Police officer): Is there any fingerprints?

Mr Aksh: No sir.

Mr Vijay (Police officer): Her friend need to tell us something. Call her for investigating.

Mr Aksh: Ok Sir.

In The Investigation Room................................

Mr Vijay (Police officer): You know very well navya. Why did we call you? That day you were saying something. Last time what happened between you two.

Navya: Last time we met in the hospital when she was injured then she fought to me for karan.

Mr Vijay (Police officer): Why did she injure and who is that Karan?

Navya: Karan is her boyfriend. Actually before that day we all meet together in the library, mostly the time shruti and karan spend time in the library. We were just talking and suddenly Shelf fell on shruti so she hospitalized for the minor injured but in the hospital Karan confessed to me that he likes me but not shruti. That's what she heard and in the end she told me that she will do anything to make him mine. And next day this happened.

Mr Vijay (Police officer): So you are trying to say that shruti suicide actually because of karan. But where is karan now. Is that karan study in your college?

Navya: Yes sir, He studied at our college. I tried to call him but his number getting switch off continuously.

Mr Vijay (Police officer): What more information you have about him?

Navya: He works at a part time job, but I don't know where he works.

Mr Vijay (Police officer): Thanks for your information we will look into it. You can go now.

Mr Vijay (Police officer): Mr Aksh, We need to go to college. Let's find who is this Karan.

In The College..

Principle: Welcome sir but how can I help you?

Mr Vijay (Police officer): We are here looking for student study in the first year of arts. His name is Karan. We need information of him.

Principle: Sure Sir let me give some time.

Sorry Sir but we can't find it.

Mr Vijay (Police officer): Let me look. So one page is already torn. Who can do this?

Principle: We are not sure who can do this in our office.

Mr Vijay (Police officer): We need to go to the library where they meet mostly there.

In The Library...

Receptionist: How can I help you sir?

Mr Vijay (Police officer): Can you tell me? How many students visit in Library? Do you have records of them?

Receptionist: Approx 1000 students because our college library also considered as city library. We collect records for students who have rent books from our library.

Mr Vijay (Police officer): So can you tell us that, Have Karan name boy ever rent any books? He mostly times a visit here.

Receptionist: Let me check sir. Sorry sir we don't have any of this.

Mr Vijay (Police officer): Have you ever seen any guy visit mostly here with this girl name shruti. Here is the picture of Shruti. Have any guy visit with her?

Receptionist: Sorry sir I have never seen her.

Mr Vijay (Police officer): Before some days, a girl injured here because book shelf fell on her but there was no one at time here why?

Receptionist: We have also heard that but actually, at every Saturday we have culture programme in our college and because of that mostly students become busy and also the part time workers get busy to arrange things for cultural activities that day.

Mr Vijay (Police officer): So you are saying that day was Saturday.

Receptionist: Yes sir.

Mr Vijay (Police officer): Don't you have CCTV?

Receptionist: Sorry Sir, actually someone already broke CCTV.

Mr Vijay (Police officer): What kind of management is this?

Receptionist: Sorry Sir.

In The Classroom................................

Mr Vijay (Police officer): Have you ever seen any guy with student name shruti?

Students: Sorry sir actually mostly the time we have seen shruti and navya together, they look like best friend and both girls never try to talk to others. Sorry sir we don't know any karan as we never talked to shruti before. She never tried to talk to others, so we don't know what was going with her life.

Mr Vijay (Police officer): It's ok. Thank you helping us.

In The Investigation Room:

Mr Aksh: How possible is this that nobody ever seen karan?

Mr Vijay (Police officer): It may be possible because karan attended classes very less because he needed to do part time and even students are also saying that shruti didn't talk that much to other students and don't share her personal life with others except navya.

Mr Aksh: We have got something about navya and shruti. Students told us that they were in same school before even their admission information also like that they were in same school before.

Mr Vijay (Police officer): We need to visit to navya. Only she can tell us more about Karan. Tell Cartoon artist to come. We need navya to tell how that karan looks like.
(Mr Vijay went to the hostel to meet navya but navya wasn't there and they came back to the police station)

Mr Aksh: Calling navya on mobile.......... ringing...

Navya: Hello, sir, how can I help you?

Mr Aksh: Can you come to police station to make a stretch of Karan.

Navya: Sure Sir.

Navya help police to make a skretch of karan.

Mr Vijay (Police officer): How many times have you seen karan?

Navya: Not many times because I haven't spend time with him. I have only met him when shruti invited him. Last time at the hospital, library and when we three night out. That day also karan was acting strange. Instead of shruti, he was trying to help to get soft drinks and to try to flirt with me.

Mr Vijay (Police officer): So you are trying to say that karan was not trustworthy. You went both together to but soft drinks, where?

Navya: I think he was not trustworthy. We went to market near our college.

Mr Vijay (Police officer): Thank you for your help, if we need any help we call you again.

Navya: Sure sir.

Mr Vijay (Police officer): Mr Aksh, Let's go to the market.

Mr Aksh: Sure Sir.

In The Market..

Shopkeeper: How can I help you Sir?

Mr Vijay (Police officer): You have CCTV in your shop. We need to check it.

Shopkeeper: Sure Sir.

Mr Vijay (Police officer): play the CCTV at the day when karan, navya and shruti was spending night out.

(In CCTV, a guy came to the shop and buy soft drinks.)

Mr Aksh: Sir, that guy in camera wore mask and coat. How will we identify his face?

Mr Vijay (Police officer): Have you found anything strange about this guy?

Shopkeeper: No, I couldn't able to see his face because of his mask but his behavior was normal. He came buy soft drinks and paid by cash.

Mr Vijay (Police officer): Thank you for your help sir.

In The Police Station..

Mr Aksh: Nothing works sir even after visiting shop.

Mr Vijay (Police officer): Something is missing. Let's check the pictures of shruti at the day of the incident. Have you got the CCTV at the day of an incident.

Mr Aksh: Yes Sir

Mr Vijay (Police officer): Let's watch it.

(In CCTV, shruti is coming to her hostel room and then after CCTV footage are missing.)

Mr Aksh: Sir something is strange if she suicided then why CCTV footage of that day need to be miss.

Mr Vijay (Police officer): Something is really strange. It doesn't look like suicide.

Wait a minute......................

When shruti was entering to her hostel room, she wasn't wearing any watch at her right hand but when she was collapsed after that incident she was wearing a watch. That was day of shruti's birthday too.

Mr Aksh: Her watch is looking made from animals leather.

Mr Vijay (Police officer): I have also noticed it and that brand is also so unique and sell at the very limited base.

Mr Aksh: When we checked shruti's hostel room, we didn't find any watch accessories or any accessories relate to animals leather. It looks like she didn't use any animal leather products.

Mr Vijay (Police officer): I know someone who has been using animal leather around shruti. We need to ask to the students again.

Mr Aksh: So sir you are trying to say that someone may be at that day visit at shruti's room and gifted her animal leather watch to shruti, that's why shruti was not wearing any watch at the time of entering her room but at time of her collapsed, she had that watch wore at her right hand.

Mr Vijay (Police officer): That's what I am imaging right now but need to be sure.

Mr Aksh: Are you suspecting someone?

Mr Vijay (Police officer): Before that I need to be sure something.

Let's go.................................

Mr Aksh: Why are we at shruti's school?

Mr Vijay (Police officer): I told you I needed to conform something.

Mr Aksh: Is this information enough?

Mr Vijay (Police officer): We need to to find the owner of that watch. Find out who sell animal leather products specially relate to that watch.

Mr Aksh: Ok Sir

Next Day...

Mr Aksh: Sir this seller who sells animal leather watches and other products too.

Mr Vijay (Police officer): Let's go there.

In The Market..

Shopkeeper: How can we help you sir?

Mr Vijay (Police officer): Do you sell this type of animal shelter watches?

Shopkeeper: Yes Sir, We basically deals with animal shelter products but we sell at very limited bases because of it's price range.

Mr Vijay (Police officer): Can we get information of those purchaser of this watch.

Shopkeeper: Sure Sir, Let me check.
Sir these are names of the purchasers.

Mr Aksh: Sir, Among these names there is one anonymous purchaser.

Mr Vijay (Police officer): Who is that anonymous purchaser?

Shopkeeper: We actually don't know, that person always text us from different numbers for any orders relate to animal leather products.

Mr Vijay (Police officer): Does this watch also ordered by that anonymous person?

Shopkeeper: Yes Sir.

Mr Vijay (Police officer): How do you deliver that watch to that anonymous person? if you didn't ever get personal contact with that person.

Shopkeeper: That person always text us delivery address.

Mr Vijay (Police officer): What's that delivery address?

Shopkeeper: Let me check sir.
Parvati Education University girls hostel was the delivery address given by that person always.

Mr Vijay (Police officer): These are pictures of some other animal leather products. Does this sell from here too?

Shopkeeper: Let me see.
Yes Sir, this products are purchased by that same anonymous purchaser through text from different numbers.

Mr Vijay (Police officer): What was the delivery address?

Shopkeeper: Again, Parvati Education University girls hostel.

Mr Vijay (Police officer): Thank you for your information.

Mr Aksh: Sir What are those pictures of animal leather products? How those pictures belong to this case?

Mr Vijay (Police officer): Those pictures which I was showing, actually those animal leather products I have seen in Navya's room when we went there to ask her help to make a skretch of Karan.

Mr Aksh: So according to the shopkeeper that watch and all other animal leather products of that pictures are purchased by that same anonymous person.
So sir it means that anonymous person is Navya.

Mr Vijay (Police officer): That's what I am thinking too. This answers only navya can give us. Call her for investigation.

In The Police Station..

Mr Arun(Police Officer Senior): Have you solved the case? How is going? Did you find any clue?

Mr Vijay (Police officer): Yes sir. It will solved today. We will send report to you by today.

Mr Arun: Ok Great.

Mr Vijay (Police officer): Let's call navya. I have some question to ask her.

Mr Aksh: Sure Sir.

Navya: How can I help you sir this time?

Mr Vijay (Police officer): We tried so hard to find karan but didn't find him. Fortunately I have been become curious about your friendship with navya.

Navya: I already have told you sir that we were best friends.

Mr Vijay (Police officer): You both went to same school before. Isn't that?

Navya: Yes Sir but what's so surprising about that?

Mr Vijay (Police officer): We went to your school but find something strange about both of your friendship. We asked to the students even asked to the student of your school batch.

Navya: Then what do you get?

Mr Vijay (Police officer): They told us that shruti always tried to insult you and always get your things what you belong to.

Navya: What's so strange about it?

Mr Vijay (Police officer): There is nothing strange, sometime best friends also have sour relationship but I have also heard that you found your boyfriend cheated you with your best friend, I mean shruti was in the affair with your boyfriend but still you forgive her.

Navya: She was my best friend anyhow I need to forgive her.

Mr Vijay (Police officer): I can understand you have a big heart to forgive her. But I don't understand why did you killed your best friend?

Navya: What are you trying to say sir that I have killed shruti. I have already told you she suicided because of karan.

Mr Vijay (Police officer): Should I tell you why we didn't find any boy name of karan. Because there is no karan.

Navya: Then How will you justify all incident happened with shruti when karan was there?

Mr Vijay (Police officer): Probably In Library there was no karan, only you and shruti was there and you make that shelf fell on shruti. Even At that night only you two spend a night out. There was never any boy with you both. You just make this story and justify everyone to believe that what you are saying that actually happened.

Navya: Then how can you justify that guy, who was buying soft drinks in the shop and in the hospital too?

Mr Vijay (Police officer): This answer, I am sure you have. Maybe, you have purchased that boy to act like karan just for a moment so that all we can believe that Karan exist.

Navya: How can you be sure of your imagination?

Mr Vijay (Police officer): Let me tell you when we went to the hostel room of yours to ask you make stretch of karan. That day I have noticed something really strange in your room. Your room fulfilled with animal leather products. Curtains, purses, watches, even clothes too. You seem addicted to the animal leather products.

Navya: So how this can belong to shruti's death.

Mr Vijay (Police officer): We must tell you that we also find something strange about shruti's death. Even in postmortem says she cut her nerves but the moment we were not able to find Karan. It becomes all strange and then we have noticed that when shruti was entering to her room, she didn't wear any watch at the day of the incident but when she was collapsed she was wearing that watch. You know what's most interesting that watch made of animal leather which type of watch I have already seen in your home. That makes me a doubt on you.

We tried to find out the purchaser of that watch from the seller after all that animal leather watch sell in very limited access. And What exactly we found that purchaser was anonymous purchaser but always has a delivery address of your hostel. And what more interesting that your animal leather products in your room also sold by that seller and all delivery address is your hostel.

So all those animal products which you have in your room sold by that seller even delivery address as your hostel says the same thing that you are the owner of that watch which shruti wore at the time of that incident. Because that watch what shruti wore also sold by that same seller and delivery address is again your hostel.

Isn't that strange everything connect to you?

Navya: But even that watch belong to me what shruti wore at time of that incident. It doesn't prove that I was there at that moment.

Mr Vijay (Police officer): We have found your fingerprints in that watch with blood of shruti. Now tell us what happened at that day and why did you killed her?

Navya: I tried so hard to hide but that dam watch...............

It's true I have killed her and make a character of Karan to make everyone believe that in her life she had a boyfriend. Everything happened because of her.

Mr Vijay (Police officer): So It means all that incidents happened to shruti before you did all that.

Navya: Yes, there was no karan I did all that to make her injured. Your Imagination was correct.

Mr Vijay (Police officer): So it means you were there at the time of incident and that watch was gifted by you to shruti.

Navya: Yes, It's true I was there at that moment and gifted her that watch.

Mr Vijay (Police officer): Why did you kill her?

Navya: I was happy to give her those small injuries. It was kind of my revenge because she keeps insulted me in front of others and always tries to get what I deserve.

That day I went to her room to wish her birthday but unfortunately I shared my good news to make her jealous and make her feel that I more worthy than her so I told her that I got opportunity to publish my story then she started again to insult me that I should publish the story by her name, not mine because I have boring personality and don't deserve any fame. So she suggested me that I should write story and give her name as writer so that she can get fame but in return she will pay me salary. She was again trying to insult me.

I just got angry and hold a knife then forced her to put the knife to her hand to cut her nerves.

Mr Vijay (Police officer): Why didn't we get any fingerprint of yours in that knife?

Navya: Because I had used plastic to hold that knife.

Mr Vijay (Police officer): Sorry we didn't find any fingerprint in that watch but you confessed everything. Now you are under arrests.

Later On...

Mr Vijay (Police officer): Sir this is report of this case.

Mr Arun: Well done, you did a good job to solve it.

Mr Vijay (Police officer): Thank you sir.